The Illuminated Desert

WORDS BY

Terry Tempest Williams

ART BY

Chloe Hedden

CALLIGRAPHY BY

Chris Montague

CANYONLANDS
Natural History Association

For Annabelle Milliken, her open heart;
and for Louis Gakumba, at home in the desert

—T.T.W.

For my parents,
who raised me to love and appreciate the Earth

—C.H.

Text © 2008 by Terry Tempest Williams
Illustrations © 2008 by Chloe Hedden
All rights reserved.

www.cnha.org

Composed in the United States of America
Printed in China

FIRST IMPRESSION

ISBN 13: 978-0937407-11-3
ISBN 10: 0-937407-11-9

08   09   10   11   12   5   4   3   2   1

Library of Congress Cataloging-in-Publication Data Pending

ACKNOWLEDGEMENTS

Brooke, Rio, and the relentless, erosional wisdom of Castle Valley; Chris Montague for his elegance of script and his devotion to all things wild; Monette Tangren Clark for her eye for details in helping to create the glossary; Bill, Eleanor, and Sarah Hedden for their grounding of friendship; Mary O'Brien for her active heart; Mary Rees for her hands upon the desert; Laura Kamala for her healing grace; Anne Marie Lane, curator, Toppan Rare Book Library, who shared with me the joys of illuminated manuscripts at the University of Wyoming; Cindy Hardgrave for her vision and leadership; Sam Wainer for the power of his perceptions. Carl Brandt for bringing this book home. And to Chloe, the pleasure and privilege of this collaboration.

—TERRY TEMPEST WILLIAMS

First and foremost, I would like to thank my coconspirator, Terry Tempest Williams, for the honor of working with her on this project. It is not often you have the opportunity to make art side-by-side with someone you admire so much— a blessing I will be slow to forget. I am also deeply grateful to my family for their support and encouragement, my partner Gabriel for his love, and the desert and all its inhabitants for inspiring this book. Chris Montague's remarkable calligraphy was a central part of the earliest vision for these pages and the experience of working with such a patient artist no less rewarding. I am enormously indebted to Cindy Hardgrave and Sam Wainer of Canyonlands Natural History Association who believed in the project, seeing the potential in just a few early paintings. I would also like to thank David Jenney for his elegant design and Theresa Howell for her meticulous editing. Mary O'Brien, Mary Rees and Tim Graham helped me accurately portray the desert; any remaining mistakes are mine. Thanks to Robert J. Valentino whose photograph of a mountain lion and its kitten was the reference for "M," and to Monette Clark and Bill Hedden for their research on the glossary. Finally, I would like to thank Bill and Pam Godschalx for their exquisite photography.

—CHLOE HEDDEN

Song of the waters calling: come and drink.
Come, all you creatures, to the shadowy brink
in dark of night.

"Song of the Soul "
—St. John of the Cross (1542–1591)

INTRODUCTION

Once Upon A Time,

books were made by hand and painted on parchment instead of paper. The finest books were bound in leather with metal hinges and locks to keep the precious contents secret and safe.

What was inside? Prayers and calendars made for spring and fall festivals, even the words spoken from the altars of churches called "the liturgy" were printed on these pages of taut calfskin.

Each letter of each word was drawn by a sharpened quill feather, dipped in ink, and held by a steady hand. Margins were filled with flowers, roses, irises, and pansies painted on gold or silver borders that shimmered in candlelight. Some pages appeared with animals sitting inside letters, next to words, a rabbit, a deer, or a wolf, framed inside elegant windows that held the sacred texts. Bluebirds and falcons flew in between paragraphs. Butterflies and moths were not uncommon visitors on the page. Even bats made appearances.

Many of these books honored the creation of a miraculous world where the stories of Jesus and the Mother Mary were told. Saints and sinners all had their place inside these richly embellished devotions. In medieval days, a book like this was known as a "Book of Hours."

The Illuminated Desert is patterned after these illuminated manuscripts. Consider it a naturalist's book of prayers, a collection of episodes, seen by two students of the natural world.

We have organized the book you now hold in your hands as an "abecedarian," a book that is arranged in alphabetical order. It is a book of discovery to see if you can find all the plants, animals, geologic curiosities, constellations, and earthly inhabitants that begin with the first letter painted on each page. A glossary at the end of the book provides natural histories to accompany the small devotions of the desert alphabet.

The Colorado Plateau, located in the Four Corners region of the American Southwest where Utah, Colorado, New Mexico, and Arizona share a common meeting point, is the focus of our inquiry and imagination. It is a landscape so startling, so fragile and enduring, at once, it can bring one to their knees in humility and awe.

The Illuminated Desert is light and poetry to be shared in the spirit of celebration.

— TERRY TEMPEST WILLIAMS
and CHLOE HEDDEN
Castle Valley, Utah

Antelope;
pronghorn;
lightning across sage;
When they run —
Wind Gods smile.

Basket-maker,
Ancient One, sits on sandstone weaving—
The Birthing Rock behind her.

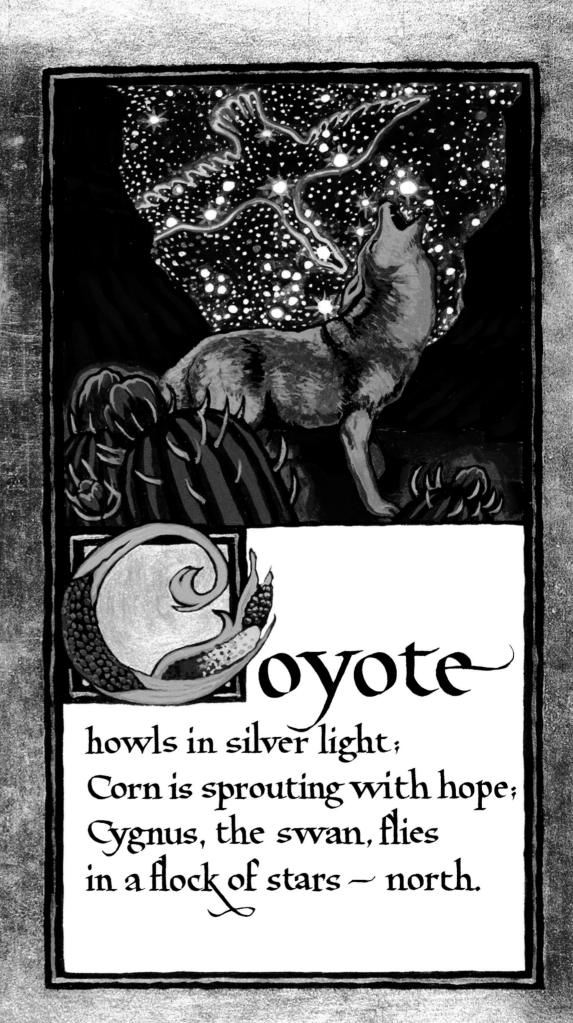

Coyote

howls in silver light;
Corn is sprouting with hope;
Cygnus, the swan, flies
in a flock of stars – north.

Datura

unfurls like a dream – the
door to night magic opens;
White-robed moth enters –
Dawn delivers daylight
in stillness.

Elk bugles at
the moment of eclipse;
on the edge of the forest,
a harem gathers;
evening primroses bloom.

Fawn
sleeps,
disturbed by nightmares
of fires and floods,
but awakens calm
to the warm nudge
of its mother.

olden
eagle
grips gopher
snake with its talons;
gila monster hides;
somewhere
ghost gourds are rattling.

Heron

eyes   a humpback chub
in the current of the Colorado—
the long-legged bird
                    steps forward;
the humpback chub is gone.

ris,
Indian paintbrush;
gardens in the desert,
draw insects toward
nectar, and bees
intoxicated on pollen.

Jack-rabbit

jumps, bounds,
zigzags through sage,
finding sanctuary in
juniper; Coyote is left
wandering, still hungry.

Kachinas
inside their kivas
keep the stories
of their people-safe.
Kit foxes, outside,
ears forward, listen.

Lizard languishes
in desert heat — lightning
strikes; thunder plays.
Rain is a downpouring
of prayers, as we walk a
labyrinth of stones.

Meteors

flash across the
Milky Way; moonlight stalks
mountain lions in peace;
monarchs rest in milkweed.

Night-hawks

nearby cry
veering right and left—
Now, afternoon light in the
narrows settles like a flame.

Owl
belongs to the night;
Otter belongs to water;
Oriole creates a cradle,
a nest unlike all others.

Prairie Dog is displaced from her village. New houses for humans rise. Petroglyphs are quiet witnesses.

Quick-sand

by the river
becomes a question of safety-
Quail call quietly from the oak.
People floating on a raft, move on.

Rattlesnake

coils in redrocks –
a warning that risk is real.
Raven plays in the shadows
dressed in drapes of darkness.

now~storms *surprise* swallows in spring. They soar above the slickrock trusting sunshine returns.

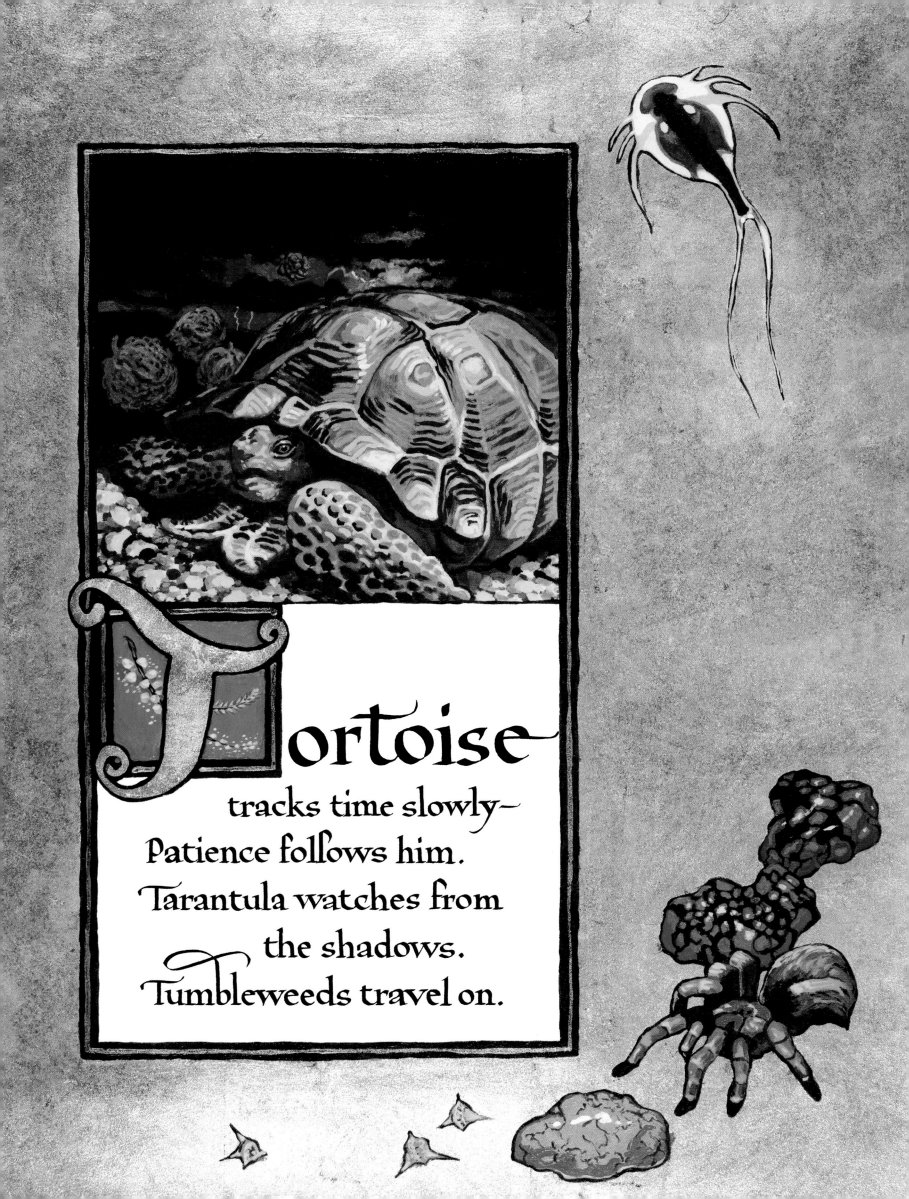

Tortoise

tracks time slowly~
Patience follows him.
Tarantula watches from
the shadows.
Tumbleweeds travel on.

Ursa Major

is the Big Dipper;
is the bear on the Earth
who inspires Ute Indians
to dance.
Life sings through circles.

Vultures view death from the vantage of sky— circling down—they descend toward decay.

Water is the signature of the illuminated desert; wrens and warblers sing along willows where life is woven together.

Xeri-scaping

is an act of kindness
where native plants are
nurtured in place and water
is not wasted on lawn~

Yucca

blooms like a candle
in the canyon, calling
night moths forward
to pollinate the future~

Zuni

are desert dwellers. The corn they plant and the fetishes they carve become offerings to the Earth.

GLOSSARY

ALPENGLOW—a reddish glow that adorns mountain peaks and redrock cliffs before sunrise or after sunset on a clear day.

ALTOCUMULUS CLOUDS—large, rounded masses of water vapor that form when an advancing cold front lifts the air on its front edge. They warn of approaching afternoon thunderstorms.

ANT (*Family Formicidae*)—small insects that evolved from wasps over 100 million years ago, and are among the most widespread organisms on Earth. Highly developed social insects, they form large, complex colonies where each individual has a specialized role.

ANTILOCAPRA AMERICANA (Pronghorn)—an elegant hoofed, grazing mammal of the grasslands of the American West. Though often called an antelope, it is rather, the only surviving member of the family Antilocapridae. Pronghorns are the fastest land animals on the North American continent.

ANTLERS—bony growths that form each year on the heads of male deer and elk. The growing antlers are supplied with nutrients by a covering of skin called velvet; this sloughs off when the antlers reach the proper size, leaving dead bone that forms the mature antler.

ARCH—a hole through a rock wall caused by the erosive forces of wind, rain, and ice.

ARROW—a slender projectile shot from a bow. Arrows have been used by most cultures since before recorded history.

ASPEN (*Populus tremuloides*)—one of the most widespread trees in North America, with white distinctive trunks, black knots, and small shimmering green leaves that quake with the wind. The leaves turn golden in autumn.

BADGER (*Taxidea taxus*)—a carnivorous mammal of the grasslands and deserts, related to ferrets, weasels, and otters. It uses claws to dig for gophers and ground squirrels. Solitary and aggressive.

BASKET—a container made of interwoven materials, such as willow, yucca, or grasses. Woven in a great variety of designs and shapes depending on their usage and the people who are making them.

BASKETMAKER—The Basketmaker culture developed around 1,500 B.C. and lasted until about 500 A.D. These people gradually made the transition from a nomadic way of life to a more settled existence as farmers. They are known for making baskets and other woven articles, such as sandals and matts.

BIGHORN SHEEP (*Ovis canadensis nelsoni*)—found throughout the southwestern deserts in steep, rough country that offers protection from predators, including man. Their name celebrates the large curved horns of the males, or rams. They graze on grasses and browse shrubs.

BIRTHING ROCK—a large boulder south of Moab, Utah, that has a petroglyph seeming to depict a birthing scene. It was probably made by an artist of the Fremont culture of native peoples who lived in the Colorado Plateau region between 700 A.D. and 1,300 A.D.

BISON (*Bison bison*)— the largest land mammal in North America. Once estimated in the millions, bison were hunted nearly to extinction by white men in the 19th century. They exist today, largely in protected areas. A small herd lives in the Henry Mountains in Utah.

BLACK BEAR (*Ursus americanus*)— the most common species of bear in North America. Prefers forests and is omnivorous, eating vegetation, fruits and berries, grubs and insects, fish, and small mammals.

BOWL—a deep rounded container or dish with an open top used to hold water, food, or seeds.

BUTTE—a landform caused by erosion of a hill having a table-like top layer that is harder than the underlying earth; a small mesa. Buttes gradually erode into narrow towers or spires before collapsing.

Canyon—a narrow cleft between high rock cliffs. Canyons may be carved by a stream flowing through, or they can be larger fractures in the rock.

Claret Cup Cactus (*Echinocereus triglochidiatus*)—the most widespread variety of hedgehog cactus. Claret cups grow on rocky soils in deserts. In spring, they produce brilliant scarlet flowers. Rather than being pollinated by insects like most cacti, claret cups are pollinated by hummingbirds.

Constellation—a grouping of stars. The actual stars in the group may be quite distant from one another in space, but their arrangement as seen from Earth suggests a human, animal, or divine form to viewers. The names of many constellations are derived from the Zodiac and Greek mythology.

Corn (*Zea mays*)—an American cereal plant of the grass family, with the grain borne on cobs enclosed in husks.

Coyote (*Canis latrans*)—a member of the dog family, native to North America. An omnivore who eats small animals, plants, and carrion. Coyote is an important character in many Native American cultures, appearing as "The Trickster" in their stories.

Cutthroat Trout (*Oncorhynchus clarki*)—a salmonid fish; varieties of cutthroats are the only native trout of the Southwest. It gets its name from "cut throat" markings, typically a red or orange slash located on either side of the lower jaw.

Cygnus—a constellation in the Milky Way which resembles a swan facing north. It is named after a king in Greek mythology who was changed into a swan.

Datura (*Datura sp.*)—moonflower; also known as "sacred datura" for the visions it can produce. The leaves and seeds contain hallucinogenic substances that can be toxic. The large white trumpet flowers bloom at night and are pollinated by moths, beetles, and wasps.

Dawn—moment when the sun crests the mesa and first light appears.

Deer, Mule (*Odocoileus hemionus*)—hoofed mammals native to western North America. Deer migrate from warmer, lower elevations in winter, to higher elevations in summer. They graze on grasses in the summer and browse on bitterbrush in fall and winter. The males grow antlers for the fall mating season.

Douglas Fir (*Pseudotsuga menziesii*)—a large conifer native to western North America, it has short, flattened needles and cones that look as though mouse-tails have been caught inside.

Dove, Mourning (*Zenaida macroura*)—a swift flying, grayish dove of North America. Named for its plaintive call.

Eclipse—a partial or total obscuring of one celestial body by another. A solar eclipse is seen when the moon blocks our view of the sun, and a lunar eclipse is observed when the earth's shadow is cast on the moon.

Elk, Rocky Mountain (*Cervus canadensis*)—a large native deer of western North America. Migrating seasonally from lower to higher elevations, elk live in grasslands, forests, and semi-deserts. Males, or bulls, grow enormous antlers each year. An elk bugling in autumn is one of the primal calls of the wild.

Ephedra, Mormon Tea (*Ephedra viridis*)—a shrubby plant native to deserts of the Southwest. The plant is a source of the chemical ephedrine and has been used as a medicinal plant by many native peoples. Mormon pioneers brewed a bitter tea from the plant, rich in vitamin C.

Evening Primrose (*Oenothera sp.*)—a signature plant of the desert, its waxy flowers, which are yellow, pink, or white, typically open in the evening. The leaves form a rosette at ground level. Pollinated by moths and specialized species of bees.

Fairy Shrimp (*Branchinecta packardi* and *Streptocephalus texanus*)—tiny, 0.5 to 1.5 inch, transparent freshwater crustaceans. They generally swim upside-down. Found in pools and potholes that may be dry for long periods of time; their eggs, or cysts, will survive drought and only hatch during favorable conditions following rainstorms.

Falcon, Peregrine (*Falco peregrinus*)—"Peregrine" means "wanderer." They have one of the longest migrations of any bird in North America. When they swoop, or dive to kill prey, they tuck back their wings and become a deadly force in the air. In the 1960s, peregrines became endangered due to DDT poisoning. Recovery efforts restored populations, taking them off the Endangered Species List in 1999.

Fall—autumn; the time of year when aspens turn yellow, maples turn red, and leaves fall from the trees. During this season, the days get shorter and cooler; the nights get longer.

Fawn—a baby deer. Newborns weigh 6-8 pounds. The mothers give birth in late spring after a 200–day gestation period, usually to twins. Lack of scent and spotted coloration helps fawns blend into underbrush, but their main defense against predators is hiding.

Feathers—the light, flat growths forming the plumage of birds. They have numerous slender, closely arranged parallel barbs that form a vane on either side of a horny, partly hollow shaft. Feathers allow birds to fly and also keep them warm and dry.

FINCH, Cassin's (*Carpodacus cassinii*)—small, seed-eating birds that include cardinals, grosbeaks, goldfinches, and sparrows, all having a short, stout bill perfectly adapted for cracking seeds.

FLASH FLOOD—a rapid flooding of low-lying areas, rivers and streams caused by intense rainfall. These rushing walls of water occur when the ground becomes saturated so quickly that it cannot be absorbed.

FOREST FIRE—an uncontrolled fire in a wooded area. Wildfires are also common in grasslands and scrublands. They tend to be most common and severe during years of drought. Wildfires are a natural part of the ecosystem of wildlands.

FREMONT COTTONWOOD (*Populus fremontii*)—a lowland type of poplar tree that is among the largest deciduous trees in the southwestern United States. Named after famed western explorer John C. Fremont, they grow in moist soil and are indicators of permanent water.

FROG, Northern Leopard (*Lithobates pipiens*)—a greenish brown carnivorous frog with large black spots and a white belly. Pollution and habitat destruction have drastically reduced their numbers. Look for them along slow moving streams.

GHOST—referring to the pictographs painted on the rock art panel known as "The Great Gallery" in Horseshoe Canyon, Utah. This impassable canyon was previously called Barrier Canyon. The unique, ancient rock art on its walls is said to be in the Barrier Canyon style.

GILA MONSTER (*Heloderma suspectum*)—a stout-bodied and venomous lizard of the desert. Covered with scales of yellow, orange, pink, and black, they have a beaded appearance. Habitat is restricted to areas near the lower Colorado River. Gila monsters are a "threatened or endangered" species in Utah and New Mexico.

GOLDEN EAGLE (*Aquila chrysaeto*)—a large majestic bird of prey native to the Northern Hemisphere, distinguished by golden feathers on the back of the head and neck. It feeds on rodents, small mammals and reptiles, mates for life, and builds large nests in canyons.

GOPHER SNAKE (*Pituophis melanoleucus*)—a non-venomous snake native to the Interior West. Its preferred food is rodents, which it kills through constriction. Light brown in color with rows of black, brown, or reddish blotches, the gopher snake can grow to be four feet long. Aggressive when disturbed, it will imitate a rattlesnake to scare off predators.

GOURD—a fruit with a hard rind, related to pumpkins and squash. Gourds come in many unusual shapes and are very durable when aged. Used by many cultures throughout time as decorative bowls, drinking vessels, and musical instruments.

HERON, Great Blue (*Ardea herodias*)—a tall, thin, wading bird with a gray-blue body and white head with long black plumes. Seen in shallow water searching for prey, the heron spears fish and frogs with its long bill and swallows them whole. In flight, great blue herons are unmistakable with their neck pulled in, and their long legs trailing behind.

HONEYBEE (*Apis mellifera*)—a small, winged, hairy-bodied, social insect that lives in colonies or hives, where each individual has a special job. Honeybees create their food from the nectar and pollen of flowers. In the process of collecting pollen, they also pollinate the flowers they visit. Vulnerable to pesticides.

HONEYCOMB—a hexagonal (six-sided) wax structure made by worker bees to to store honey, eggs, larvae, and pollen.

HUMMINGBIRD, Black-chinned (*Archilochus alexandri*)—tiny birds with long, tubular bills that feed on nectar and small insects. Bifurcated (forked) tongues help them sip nectar deep within red, slender flowers. Hummingbirds beat their wings rapidly, up to 1,260 beats per minute. They weave tiny nests out of spider webs, feathers, and horse hair.

HUMPBACK CHUB (*Gila cypha*)—an endangered fish that lives only in the Colorado River. It needs the silty water of spring floods to breed. A large hump on their backs helps them hold their position in the fast flowing currents of the river.

INCHWORM—the common name for larvae of the moths belonging to the family *Geometridae*. Because inchworms are missing legs on the middle section of the abdomen, as they "inch" forward on a twig, they create a shape with their bodies that resembles the Greek letter Omega.

INDIAN PAINTBRUSH (*Castilleja angustifolia*)—a stunning wildflower with a bushy spike of clustered red, orange, yellow, or white blossoms. Many species. Grows in varied habitats from 2000′ to 8000′ elevation. Removes selenium (toxins) from the soil.

INDIAN RICE GRASS (*Achnatherum hymenoides*)—the native, state grass of Utah; grows in drought tolerant bunches. Seed heads provide food for many animals and birds. Native peoples made flour from the nutritious seeds. Its significance is represented by a petroglyph in Canyonlands National Park, in which a spirit figure holds a shock of rice grass.

INSECTS (*Class Insecta*)—a diverse classification of animals identified by a hard external skeleton, three body sections, (head, thorax, and abdomen), six legs, a single pair of antennae, wings, and compound eyes.

IRIS, Rocky Mountain (*Iris missouriensis*)—a small perennial wild iris resembling its domestic cousins. The purple to blue flowers are found from the foothills to the mountains, especially in meadows. The length of time that the iris blooms is determined by the spring rains.

JACKRABBIT, Black-tailed *(Lepus californicus)*—not actually a rabbit, but a hare. Strong back legs allow it to outrun predators, such as coyotes and foxes. Large ears create keen hearing and when flapped, dissipate desert heat.

JERUSALEM CRICKET *(Stenopelmatus fuscus)*—a heavyset cricket of the dry country with a large head, well-suited to eating other insects.

JUNE BUG *(Phyllophaga sp.)*—a large scarab beetle that appears in early summer, often flying into outdoor lights. It is a scavenger, important for recycling dung and dead creatures, both plant and animal.

JUNIPER, Utah *(Juniperus osteosperma)*—a bushy evergreen that is the most common tree in Utah, forming wood-lands with pinon pines. With their twisted gray trunks and masses of blue seed "berries," junipers provide important cover and food for birds, squirrels, rabbits, and coyotes.

JUPITER—the largest planet in the solar system, made primarily of hydrogen and helium gasses; named after the king of the Roman gods.

KACHINA—a powerful spirit within Hopi religious life. Male dancers wearing masks of individual Kachinas perform seasonal dances and ceremonies to evoke their specific personalities and gifts. Wooden dolls, carved from the root of a cottonwood tree, honor a particular Kachina spirit.

KANGAROO RAT *(Dipodomys deserti)*—a nocturnal rodent with large eyes, a long tail, and extra-long legs. It can jump from place to place balanced by its tail, like a little kangaroo, sometimes covering up to 6 feet in a single leap. It gets its water from the seeds it eats.

KIT FOX *(Vulpes macrotis)*—the only true desert fox, cat-like in appearance, with oversized ears, and a narrow face. The long, bushy tail is about one third of its total size. Fierce predators, they hunt jackrabbits, kangaroo rats, ground-nesting birds, and insects.

KIVA—a circular underground chamber used by Puebloan cultures for ceremonies imparting wisdom from the elders. To enter, one climbs down a ladder made with long poles pointing skyward.

LABYRINTH—an ancient architectural structure built on the ground that offers an intricate, meditative pathway to the center and back out again. The Hopi use a particular motif called "Man in the Maze" in their silverwork and on baskets, representative of the path we walk in life.

LEDGE—a flat shelf of rock protruding from a cliff or slope. The walls above sandstone ledges are often good places to look for petroglyphs and pictographs or the remnants of cliff dwellings.

LIGHTNING—an electrical spark or zig-zag of light discharged in the atmosphere during a thunderstorm. This dramatic flash of light illuminates buttes and mesas on stormy nights.

LIZARD, Collared *(Crotaphytus collaris)*—a charismatic lizard that poses on boulders. The male has a bright yellow head with black bands that appear as necklaces. It has a green and turquoise body with yellow stripes. Orange spots may adorn the shoulders. Capable of running a hundred yard dash on its hind legs.

MESA—a small, isolated plateau with steep sides and a flat top.

METEORS—often called shooting stars, meteors are chunks of rocks and ice that enter the earth's upper atmosphere from outer space and burn up as they fall to the surface. A meteor shower occurs when the Earth passes through the tail of a comet. Nowhere is a meteor shower more dramatic than in the dark clarity of a desert night.

MILKWEED *(Asclepias tuberosa)*—a hearty plant with opposite leaves, pink flowers in a cluster, and long textured pods that split open to release seeds with downy tufts that float on the wind. When cut, exudes a milky juice. It attracks monarch butterflies.

MILKWEED BEETLE *(Tetraopes sp.)*—a small red, black-spotted beetle with long antennae; lives on milkweed plants.

MONARCH BUTTERFLY *(Danaus plexippus)*—a butterfly with bright orange wings veined in black and bordered by white spots. Monarchs migrate from the United States to the mountains of Mexico.

MONARCH CATERPILLAR—the brightly striped yellow, black, and white larvae of the monarch butterfly; it feeds on the leaves of milkweed in late summer and early fall.

MONARCH CHRYSALIS—the pale green and gold, hard-shelled pupa of the monarch butterfly, from which an adult butterfly will emerge with folded, wet wings.

MOON—the celestial body that revolves around the Earth in approximately 28 days and accompanies us in our yearly revolution around the sun. At 238,357 miles from Earth, the moon's gravitational pull influences ocean tides.

MOONLIGHT—sunlight reflected from the moon.

MOUNTAINS—the high points of the Earth's surface rising steeply to summits usually more than 2000 feet above the sea.

MOUNTAIN LION *(Felis concolor)*—the "cat of one color" is a common predator on the Colorado Plateau. Its elusive and nocturnal habits, however, make it one of the most rarely seen animals in the desert. The mountain lion's favorite food is mule deer. Mother lions purr and chirp with kittens that may stay with them for up to two years.

NARROWS—a slot canyon that is taller than it is wide, formed by water rushing through rock.

NECTAR—a sweet liquid secreted by flowers that attracts bees, butterflies, and birds, and can aid in pollination.

NIGHTHAWKS, Common (*Chordeiles minor*)—birds in the family of Caprimulgidae, sometimes called "goatsuckers," who share a well-camouflaged plumage known as a "dead leaf pattern." The nighthawk's cry in the desert is a familiar nasal sound heard overhead. They have large eyes, adapted for night vision, and wide mouths equipped with bristles for catching insects on the wing.

OASIS—a lush, green, fertile place in the desert, created by water.

OLIVE, Russian (*Elaeagnus angustifolia*)—a non-native shrub found within the Colorado Plateau that is between 12 and 45 feet tall. It can grow up to six feet a year, choking out native riparian vegetation such as willows and cottonwoods.

ORIOLE, Bullock's (*Icterus bullockii*)—a bird in the family *Enberizidae* with a sharp-pointed bill and brightly colored plumage. Northern orioles have an orange face, black crown, and yellow body with black and white wings. They weave a basket-like nest that is suspended from the branches of trees.

ORION—the great warrior in Greek mythology who is one of the most recognizable constellations in the night sky. It is easily identified by three bright stars, closely aligned, said to be Orion's belt. This constellation can be seen in both the northern and southern hemispheres.

OTTER (*Lontra Canadensis*)—a powerful swimmer and playful mammal, otters belong to the *Mustelidae* family, which includes weasels and badgers. They eat fish, insects, and frogs. Active at dusk and dawn, a group of otters is known as a "romp."

OWL, Great Horned (*Bubo virginianus*)—a nocturnal bird of prey that belongs to the family *Strigidae*. Powerful hunter who relies on the softness of its feathers to create a silent attack on rodents and rabbits. Great horned owls nest in cottonwood trees. Their "horns" are actually upright feathers.

PETROGLYPH—a type of rock art created by pecking or scratching on stone, commonly found on the dark "desert varnish" surface of cliff faces. These figures and motifs were created by prehistoric and historic peoples over thousands of years. Rock art within the Colorado Plateau has been produced by Ancestral Puebloan (Anasazi), Fremont, and Ute people dating back as far as 1200 years ago.

PICTOGRAPH—a type of rock art created by painting or drawing on rocks. Many of the colors used have been made from mineral pigments and plant dyes. They are often found in association with petroglyphs and were created by the same ancient and historic peoples within the Colorado Plateau.

PINYON JAY (*Gymnorhinus cyanocephalus*)—a bird in the family *Corvidae*, that also includes other jays, crows, and ravens. Grey-blue with a long, sharp bill and a short stubby tail, about the size of a robin. Eats the seeds of pinyon pines. In the fall, it will store the seeds, recalling where each seed cache is during the winter.

PINYON PINE (*Pinus edulis*)—a 10 to 30 foot evergreen that grows in the shape of a pyramid. Needles are 1 to 2 inches long, arranged in a spiral, with two needles in each cluster. Seeds are known as pine nuts, a valuable food for animals, birds, and humans. Pinyons live in close proximity with junipers.

PLEIADES—a cluster of stars found inside the constellation Taurus, the Bull. They are said to represent the seven daughters of Atlas and Pleione, placed by Zeus in the night sky. The Diné, or Navajo, call them "Dilyehe, translated as "Sparkling Particles."

PORCUPINE (*Erethizon dorsatum*)—second largest rodent in North America next to the beaver, possessing 30,000 quills, loosely attached to individual muscles beneath the skin. A nocturnal and solitary mammal, it does not shoot its quills but rather embeds them with powerful barbs.

PRAIRIE DOG (*Cynomys sp.*)—a communal rodent of the family *Scuridae*. They create intricate burrow systems and live in "prairie dog towns." With a variety of calls, they ward off predators like coyotes and badgers. A "keystone species," they create habitat for hundreds of other creatures, from burrowing owls, to rattlesnakes, to mountain plovers. Utah, white-tailed, and Gunnison prairie dogs, all threatened species, reside in the Colorado Plateau.

PRICKLY PEAR CACTUS (*Opuntia sp.*)—a cactus with a large flattened pad covered in long, sharp spines. Grows in clumps in disturbed areas of the desert. It also has clusters of tiny barbed spines, called glochids, at the base of the larger spines. Waxy blossoms are yellow and the fruit edible.

QUAIL, Gambel's (*Callipepla gambelii*)—a partridge-like bird often found foraging in the underbrush of oak. Males have a black throat with a top knot on their heads. Groups of 20 or more are called a "covey."

QUARTZ—a transparent mineral made from silicon dioxide and oxygen, the two most common chemical elements in the Earth. Quartz crystal is found in all types of igneous, metamorphic, and sedimentary rocks. Most sands are weathered fragments of quartz.

QUEEN BEE—the only fertile female bee; at the center of the hive she is fed royal jelly by worker bees and lays eggs fertilized by the drones. Belongs to the honey bee family *Apoidea*. Seldom seen.

QUICKSAND—a pocket of loose, wet, deep sand usually near the banks of a river, whereby a person or animal can easily be engulfed, trapped, stuck.

QUILL—a large, stiff wing feather of a bird that can be used as a writing instrument; also the hollow, barbed quill of a porcupine.

RAIN—water that condenses in clouds to fall to Earth in drops. In dry desert air, rain sometimes evaporates before reaching the ground, this is called "virga." Vital.

RAINBOW—an arc of colors, the full range of the prism, appearing in the sky opposite the sun. The colors are caused by the reflection and refraction of the sun's rays through drops of rain.

RAPID—a fast moving stretch of river formed where the riverbed descends steeply. In the roughest rapids, boulders in the channel block the flow, causing waves and the froth of whitewater.

RATTLESNAKE, (Crotalus sp.) (Sistrurus sp.)—a poisonous American pit viper that preys on small mammals and birds. Brown and tan diamonds run down its back, making it well camouflaged against desert sands. The tail ends in loosely attached, horny segments that create a dry rattling sound or fast buzz as the snake vibrates its tail in warning.

RAVEN (Corvus corax)—a member of the family Corvidae along with jays and crows. Jet black, with long, scraggy throat feathers, it is one of the quintessential birds of the redrock desert. Often seen soaring above the slickrock, cavorting on heat waves, it is highly intelligent, a scavenger, and according to many southwestern Indian tribes, a Trickster.

REDROCKS—sandstone rocks rich in iron oxide found throughout the Colorado Plateau.

RINGTAIL CAT (Bassariscus astutus)—nocturnal animal around 28″ from nose to tail in the raccoon family. The body is gray with a distinctive long, black and white banded tail. Most often found in riparian habitats. Preys on small mammals, birds, lizards and insects. Sometimes seen perched in cottonwood trees. Great climber.

RIVER—a well established channel that carries water from higher to lower elevations. Within the Colorado Plateau, the Colorado River, the Green River, the San Juan, Escalante, Fremont, and Virgin rivers play significant roles in the erosional and ecological life of this region.

ROSE, Wild (Rosa woodsii)—a woody shrub with pink flowers of five petals, five sepals, and numerous stamens. Rose hips are a red and waxy fruit, rich in vitamin C. Fire resistant and drought tolerant; they grow in elevations from 3,500 to 7,500 feet.

SAGE (Artemisia tridentate)—a highly branched, silver-blue shrub that belongs to the sunflower family, the signature plant of the American West. Extremely fragrant. The tip of individual leaves is 3-lobed, covered with tiny silver hairs. Small yellow flowers bloom on tall spikes in the fall. The bark shreds easily and is grey-brown. Used in ceremony by the Hopi and Diné.

SANDSTONE—a sedimentary rock made of sand particles cemented together with various materials, including silicates, iron oxides, calcite, and/or clay. Hardness and color varies.

SCORPION (Centruroides sp.)—a yellow, transparent creature of the class Arachnida. Around 2.5 inches long, it is venomous, inflicting a painful sting from a bulb at the tip of its arching tail. Nocturnal, it preys on insects and is preyed upon by lizards and snakes.

SEDIMENTARY ROCKS—rocks formed from the accumulations of ancient seas: sand, mud, and shells cemented through time. Stratification or layering is an important characteristic of sandstone, limestones, and shales.

SEGO LILY (Calochortus nuttalli)—a white, satin-like flower with three petals in the lily family. Inside the white cup there are cherry red and yellow markings at its base. This beautiful, showy flower that blooms in spring sits on top of a thread-like stem. The bulbs are said to have saved Mormon pioneers from starvation, hence, it is Utah's state flower.

SNOW—water vapor that has frozen into ice crystals, which join together to form snowflakes that fall to the ground as precipitation.

STREAM—small body of moving water. Desert streams are of three types: perennial, which have visible water flowing year-round; intermittent, which rise according to rainfall or snowmelt; and ephemeral, which flow only in response to precipitation and otherwise are dry.

SUN—the central body around which Earth and the other planets rotate. At 93 million miles from Earth it is our closest star and 4.6 billion years old. Ancient peoples worshipped the sun as the source of life. The sun is a driving force in the desert.

SUNFLOWER (Helianthus sp.)—Greek "helio" for sun and "anthus" for flower. The name refers to the flower's habit of turning with the sun. Sunflower seeds are eaten by small rodents and birds, look for gold finches and pine siskins.

SWALLOW, Barn (Hirundo rustica)—a swift aerial bird easily identified by its navy blue back, reddish-brown throat, and deeply forked tail. Builds a cuplike nest of mud on the underside of bridges and lives in small colonies. An insectivore that spends most of its time in the air, it often dips down to the surface of lakes and rivers to drink.

SWIFT, White-throated (Aeronautes saxatalis)—a delicate, aerodynamic bird that spends most of its life in flight. It lives in redrock canyons where it builds its nest in cracks on vertical cliff faces, anchoring the grass bits and feathers with saliva. It feeds on insects, which it catches and eats in mid-air.

TAMARISK (*Tamarix ramosissima*)—also known as salt cedar, is a long-lived, highly successful, exotic, feathery shrub that grows along riverbanks, marshes and irrigation ditches throughout the arid Southwest. It is very difficult to eradicate and chokes out native species like willows and cottonwoods.

TARANTULA (*Aphonopelma sp.*)—a large hairy spider with a leg span up to 6 inches wide; much feared, though seldom bites. Waiting inside their burrows for prey to walk by, they will eat frogs, lizards, and insects. A long-lived spider, females can survive up to 25 years in the desert.

THORN, Goathead (*Tribulus terrestrus*)—also called puncturevine, the goathead is one of the West's most noxious, notorious weeds. Native to the Mediterranean region, this plant is an annual invader of roadsides, waste areas, pastures, and cultivated fields. Hard spiny seeds damage bike tires and injure livestock.

THUNDERSTORM—a localized storm produced by a cumulonimbus cloud. Characterized by strong updraft and downdraft winds, lightning, thunder, heavy rain, and sometimes hail. The rapid rise and cooling of warm, moist air creates cumulonimbus clouds, making summertime "thunderstorm season" in the southwestern deserts.

TORTOISE, Desert (*Gopherus agassizii*)—a reptile that moves slowly in the desert in its domed shell. Its head is small and rounded, eyes are greenish yellow. An endangered species due to loss of habitat and predation by ravens; it can live up to 100 years. It feeds on grasses and herbs and lives in burrows which can be 20 degrees cooler than outside its den.

TUMBLEWEED, Russian Thistle (*Salsola kali*)—an annual plant that begins green and is thorned by summer. In fall, it is uprooted, broken at the stem, and sent tumbling by the wind. Dry, branched and round in shape, tumbleweeds can be seen stacked against barbed wire fences in the American West.

UPLIFT—a raising of the level of the land. Large scale uplifts like plateaus and mountain ranges may be caused by collisions of continental plates, while smaller uplifts can occur when erosion removes so much material and weight from a particular area that the underlying rock layers rebound upward.

URANIUM (*U*)—atomic number 92. A hard, silvery, radioactive, metallic, chemical element. Southeast Utah and southwest Colorado contain large deposits of uranium, and it was heavily mined in the 1940s and 50s, during the Cold War. One of the greatest challenges within the Colorado Plateau is whether or not to continue activities that produce radioactive waste and if so, how to safely store it when it remains radioactive for tens of thousands of years.

URSUS MAJOR—Latin for "Great Bear," this constellation helps form another famous arrangement of stars: the Big Dipper. The two stars on the far wall of the dipper's bowl point to Polaris, the North Star.

UTE—Native Americans who belong to the Shoshonean people of Utah, Colorado, and northern New Mexico. Members of the Ute Tribe now live on reservations in northeastern Utah and western Colorado. Ute means "Land of the Sun," from which the state of Utah derives its name.

VARNISH, Desert—spectacular streaks of black, brown, and red can be seen, almost like paint strokes, on cliff faces of redrock canyons. They are mineral deposits made up of clay, iron, and manganese oxide. Early desert dwellers created petroglyphs on rock walls and boulders by scraping off this patina to give their signs and symbols contrast and relief.

VELVET ANT (*Dasymutilla occidentalis*)— a wasp that looks like an ant, densely covered with orange, red, yellow, or black hairs that look like "dyed tufts of cotton." It can inflict a painful sting and is often seen scurrying across the sand on its way to invading the nests of other wasps.

VIRGIN'S BOWER (*Clematis ligusticifolia*)—a woody, vined plant with tiny inconspicuous flowers whose seed heads look like cotton balls. A tea made from the white bark can be used for a wide range of herbal remedies, from chest pains to stomach aches to tired feet.

VULTURE (*Cathartes aura*)—an emblematic scavenger of the desert Southwest, with a bald red head, white hooked beak and black wings. Adapted for entering carcasses and dining on carrion, its urine contains antiseptic agents that run down its legs and cleans them, as stomach enzymes break up ingested bones.

WARBLER, Wilson's (*Wilsonia pusilla*)—a small, migratory bird native to North America. A summer desert resident, it inhabits riparian areas, especially willows. Males have olive-green bodies, yellow breasts, and a small black cap. Insect eaters.

WATER—a transparent, odorless, tasteless liquid composed of hydrogen and oxygen: H2O. Water is found in rain and gathers in oceans, lakes, and rivers. It freezes at 32 degrees Fahrenheit (0 degrees Centigrade) and boils at 212 degrees F (100 degrees C). Water is essential to all life and is particularly precious in the desert.

WATERFALL—a steep fall or flow of water in a watercourse such as a river or stream, where it pours over a cliff, or ledge, or rocks.

WEATHERING—the various processes of wearing down and breaking apart rock; through agents of change such as wind and water.

WEAVING—the process and pattern of interlacing yarns together to make a rug or piece of fabric. One of the dominant crafts of native peoples of the American Southwest. Navajo blankets are emblematic of a kind of weaving where each design pertains to a specific style and location. Many of these designs speak to the symmetry and balance found within the natural world, known as "*hozho*."

WILLOW (*Salix sp.*)—a large wispy plant characterized by narrow, lance-shaped leaves and cotton-like catkins bearing small flowers. Willows grow in thickets by the river's edge and are a pioneering species that take root after flash floods. Desert dwellers through time have used the pliable branches of willows for weaving baskets and mats.

WIND—air in motion, moving at any velocity along the Earth's surface. Wind is the relentless voice of the desert.

WOOD, Petrified—fossilized wood, created when minerals slowly replace all organic material in dead wood, leaving the original structure and appearance of wood. Petrifaction must occur underground, in the presence of mineral-rich water and the absence of oxygen. At Petrified Forest National Park in northeastern Arizona, massive petrified trunks provide evidence of a conifer forest that existed 200 million years ago.

WOODPECKER, Downy (*Picoides pubescens*)—the smallest woodpecker in North America. Similar in appearance to the Hairy Woodpecker, the Downy is black and white with a conical bill used for drilling into tree bark in search of boring insects. Males have a red patch on the back of the head. They roost in tree cavities in the winter; often seen in aspens.

WREN, Canyon (*Catherpes mexicanus*)—a small North American wren that inhabits the canyon country of southern Utah. It prefers sandstone cliffs and slickrock near water, as it probes into crevices with its long bill, feeding on insects and spiders. Rusty in color with its distinctive white throat and banded tail, it is heard more than seen. This iconic bird holds the clarion cry of the desert in its descending trill that ricochets off canyon walls.

XANTUSIIDAE, Utah Night Lizard (*Xantusia vigilis utahensis*)—a very small lizard that is not nocturnal at all, but rather hunts during the day and lives almost exclusively under yucca plants.

XERISCAPE—refers to landscaping with plants that do not require the usual amounts of water to thrive. Drought-tolerant desert plants, such as agave, cactus, juniper, and native grasses are commonly used in xeriscaping.

XEROPHYHTE—"xero" means dry and "phyte" means plant, describing plants such as prickly pear cactus or penstemens which have adapted themselves to survive in an ecosystem with little or no water.

XYLEM—the wood-like structure in vascular plants that transports water from the roots to the cells of the plants.

YARN—long, continuous fibers spun together, often used in weaving. The Diné, or Navajo, make their yarn from the wool of churro sheep. The wool is carded and spun, and later woven into their distinctive rugs.

YELLOW-BILLED CUCKOO (*Coccyzus americanus*)—a rare brown songbird with a long, narrow tail and a curved bill. Insect eater. It inhabits trees and shrubs along streams and rivers. Cuckoos occasionally lay eggs in the nests of other birds.

YELLOWJACKET (*Vespula sp.*) (*Dolichovespula sp.*)—the name given to black and yellow wasps, they live in colonies and make paper nests. The nest is started by a single queen and can become as large as a basketball. Unlike bees, wasps can sting repeatedly because their stingers don't have barbs.

YUCCA, Narrowleaf (*Yucca angustissima*)—a member of the agave family, easily identified by its tall white stalk of creamy, bell-shaped blossoms rising from a base of sword-like leaves. The state flower of New Mexico has long been used by desert dwellers for its fibers twisted into baskets, mats, and sandals; edible fruit; roots that can be pounded and used as soap.

YUCCA MOTH (*Tegeticula yucasella*)—the small white moth that pollinates the yucca at night. The female enters an individual blossom, rolls the pollen inside into a ball, and then carries it to the next blossom. There, she lays her eggs inside the yucca's ovaries with the pollen ball rolled next to the flower's stigma, which will one day become seeds, ensuring that her young will have something to eat. This benefits both plant and progeny.

ZEA MAYS—corn, also called maize. Many Pueblo people grow corn in the desert with little water and a digging stick. Both eaten and used in ceremonies.

ZENITH—the highest point; a point directly overhead in the sky.

ZEPHYR—the west wind; also, a slight, gentle breeze.

ZODIAC—an imaginary circle within the heavens that includes the twelve constellations: Aries, Taurus, Gemini, Cancer, Leo, Virgo, Libra, Scorpio, Sagittarius, Capricorn, Aquarius, and Pisces.

ZOOMORPHISM—the representation of animal forms in decorative art or symbols. Animal motifs such as lizards, bears, or bighorn sheep can appear on pots, baskets, and jewelery.

ZUNI—a tribe of Pueblo people living in western New Mexico, who are peaceful farmers with a unique language and intricate cycle of religious ceremonies. Their exquisite arts and crafts are well known, especially their turquoise and silver jewelry, fetish carvings, and pottery.

BIBLIOGRAPHY

A Glossary of Geographical Terms, Sir Dudley Stamp, Ed., Longman, 2nd Ed., 1966, Green and Co., Ltd., London.

A Naturalist's Guide to Canyon Country, David Williams. A Falcon Guide, in cooperation with Canyonlands Natural History Association, 2000, Falcon Publishing, Helena, MT.

Anasazi: Ancient People of the Rock, Donald G. Pike. Special Consultant: Dr. Robert H. Lister, Director, Chaco Canyon Archaeological Center, University of NM, 1974, Harmony Books, New York.

Canyon Country Wildflowers, A Field Guide to Common Wildflowers, Shrubs, & Trees, Damian Fagan. A Falcon Guide, in cooperation with Canyonlands Natural History Association, 1998, Falcon Publishing, Helena.

Concise Animal Encyclopedia, David Burnie, 2000, Kingfisher Publications, Boston.

Cosmos, Carl Sagan, 1980, Carl Sagan Productions, Inc., Random House, New York.

Desert and Mountain Plants of the Southwest, Dorothy VanDyke Leake, John Benjamin Leake, Marcelotte Leake Roeder, 1993, U of Oklahoma Press, Norman.

Dictionary of Geological Terms, Third Edition, American Geological Institute, Robert L. Bates and Julia A. Jackson, Editors, 1984, Anchor Books, Doubleday, New York.

Easy Field Guide to Common Desert Birds, Richard and Sharon Nelson, 1996, Primer Publishers, Phoenix.

Easy Field Guide to Common Desert Insects, Richard and Sharon Nelson, 1996, Primer Publishers, Phoenix.

Field Guide to the Birds of North America, Shirley L. Scott, Ed., 2nd Ed., 1987, National Geographic Society, Washington, DC.

Guide to Familiar American Insects, Golden Nature Guide, revised Ed, 1956, Simon and Schuster, New York.

Guide to Familiar American Trees, Golden Nature Guide, 1956, Western Publishing Co, Golden Press, New York.

Introduction to the Atmosphere, Herbert Riehl, 1965, McGraw-Hill, New York.

Mammals of the Canyon Country, David M. Armstrong, 1982, Canyonlands Natural History Association, Moab, UT.

Mammals of the Central Rockies, Jan L. Wassink, 1993, Mountain Press Publishing, Missoula, MT.

Natural History of the Colorado Plateau and Great Basin, Kimball Harper, Larry St. Clair, Kaye Thorne, and Wilford Hess, Editors, 1994, University Press of Colorado, Niwot, CO.

Naturalist's Guide to the White Rim Trail - Canyonlands National Park, David Williams and Damian Fagan, 1994, Revised 1996, Wingate Ink, 157 S. 200 E., Moab, Utah.

Peterson First Guide to Astronomy, Jay M. Pasachoff, 1988, updated 1997, Houghton Mifflin, Boston.

Petroglyphs and Pictographs of Utah, Vol. One: The East and Northeast, Kenneth B. Castleton, M.D., 1984, Utah Museum of Natural History, Salt Lake City.

Rock Art of the American Southwest, Scott Thybony, Softbound Ed., 1999, Graphic Arts Center Publishing, Portland.

Rocky Mountain Safari: A Wildlife Discovery Guide, Cathy and Gordon Illg, 1994, Roberts Rinehart Publishers, Niwot, Colorado.

Scenes of the Plateau Lands and How They Came to Be, Wm. Lee Stokes, 1969, 20th Printing, 2000, Starstone Publishing, Salt Lake City.

Webster's New World Children's Dictionary, 1991, Simon & Schuster, Cleveland, OH.

Webster's New World Dictionary, Third College Edition, 1988, Simon & Schuster, Inc., New York.

Western Birds, Peterson Field Guides, Edited by Roger Tory Peterson, 3rd Edition, 1990, Houghton Mifflin Co, Boston.